Dear Parent:
Your child's love of reading starts here!

Every child learns to read in a different way and at his or her own speed. Some go back and forth between reading levels and read favorite books again and again. Others read through each level in order. You can help your young reader improve and become more confident by encouraging his or her own interests and abilities. From books your child reads with you to the first books he or she reads alone, there are I Can Read Books for every stage of reading:

SHARED READING
Basic language, word repetition, and whimsical illustrations, ideal for sharing with your emergent reader

BEGINNING READING
Short sentences, familiar words, and simple concepts for children eager to read on their own

READING WITH HELP
Engaging stories, longer sentences, and language play for developing readers

READING ALONE
Complex plots, challenging vocabulary, and high-interest topics for the independent reader

ADVANCED READING
Short paragraphs, chapters, and exciting themes for the perfect bridge to chapter books

I Can Read Books have introduced children to the joy of reading since 1957. Featuring award-winning authors and illustrators and a fabulous cast of beloved characters, I Can Read Books set the standard for beginning readers.

A lifetime of discovery begins with the magical words "I Can Read!"

Visit www.icanread.com for information
on enriching your child's reading experience.

For Grace the Baker & Farmer Fred
—H. P.

To Elynor—L. S.

The recipe for Amelia Bedelia's Sheet Cake was inspired by a recipe
in *The Cotton Country Collection,* compiled and printed by the Junior
Charity League of Monroe, Louisiana, in 1972.

ISBN 978-0-545-41574-3

Text copyright © 2010 by Herman S. Parish III.
Illustrations copyright © 2010 by Lynn Sweat. I Can Read Book® is a trademark of
HarperCollins Publishers. Amelia Bedelia is a registered trademark of Peppermint Partners,
LLC. All rights reserved. Published by Scholastic Inc., 557 Broadway, New York, NY
10012, by arrangement with HarperCollins Children's Books, a division of HarperCollins
Publishers. SCHOLASTIC and associated logos are trademarks and/or registered
trademarks of Scholastic Inc.

12 11 10 9 8 7 6 5 4 3 2 1   11 12 13 14 15 16/0

Printed in the U.S.A.   40

First Scholastic printing, September 2011

Watercolors and black ink were used to prepare the full-color art.

Amelia Bedelia Bakes Off

story by Herman Parish
pictures by Lynn Sweat

SCHOLASTIC INC.
New York Toronto London Auckland
Sydney Mexico City New Delhi Hong Kong

On her day off, Amelia Bedelia

stopped by to visit Mr. and Mrs. Rogers.

"Morning, everybody," said Amelia Bedelia.

"Shhhhh!" said Mr. Rogers.

"Sorry," said Amelia Bedelia quietly.

"Don't mind him," said Mrs. Rogers.

"He's watching his favorite show,

What's Cooking?"

"I give up," said Amelia Bedelia.

"What are you cooking?"

"Nothing," said Mrs. Rogers.

"That is the name of the program."

Mr. Rogers was getting annoyed.

"Please be quiet, for Pete's sake!"

"Who is Pete?"

Amelia Bedelia whispered.

Mrs. Rogers smiled and said,

"His name is Chef Du Jour.

He shows people how to make

gourmet meals and fancy desserts."

Mr. Rogers turned up the volume.

"Don't forget!"

Chef Du Jour was saying.

"I'll pick the winner

of my big Bake-Off contest.

The best baker will get

one thousand dollars!"

The audience applauded wildly.

Mr. Rogers clapped his hands, too.

"Wow!" he said. "A thousand bucks!

That is a lot of dough!"

"Not really," said Amelia Bedelia.

"A thousand bucks is a lot of deer,

but there is no doe at all."

"Amelia Bedelia," said Mrs. Rogers,

"you ought to enter that contest.

You make the best lemon meringue pie."

"She's right," said Mr. Rogers.

"A smart cookie would give it a try."

"Thanks anyway," said Amelia Bedelia.

"By tonight I will be all baked out.

Cousin Alcolu and I are running

Grace's Cookie Jar all day today."

"You two, run a bakery?" said Mr. Rogers.

"That sounds like a half-baked idea."

"No it isn't," said Amelia Bedelia.

"This idea is completely baked.

Grace had to go out of town.

She left us her recipes."

"You'll do fine," said Mrs. Rogers.

"Call us if you need help."

"Will do," said Amelia Bedelia.

On her way to the bakery, Amelia Bedelia

thought about smart cookies.

Did they taste better?

By the time she arrived,

Cousin Alcolu was unlocking the door.

"Hi, Cousin Alcolu," said Amelia Bedelia.

"Hey there," he said. "You look puzzled."

"I was wondering," said Amelia Bedelia.

"Can a cookie be smart?"

Cousin Alcolu shrugged his shoulders.

"A cookie can be rich," he said.

"I've heard that, too," she said.

"Is that what a fortune cookie is?"

Cousin Alcolu shrugged again and said,

"Maybe so. We'd better get started."

They went inside and got ready

to do some serious baking.

They found a big stack of recipes,

along with a note from Grace.

"This will be easy," said Amelia Bedelia.

"Grace will tell us exactly what to do."

They read her note together.

Amelia Bedelia scratched Cousin Alcolu's back.

Then Cousin Alcolu scratched her back.

"That felt good," said Amelia Bedelia.

"Now I feel like baking. What's first?"

Cousin Alcolu read from the note aloud:

"Bake a batch of chocolate chip cookies,

but cut the recipe in half."

"That's easy," said Amelia Bedelia.

Cousin Alcolu shook his head.

"You know," said Amelia Bedelia,

"I guess we ought to cut all of the

chocolate chips in half, too."

"What?" said Cousin Alcolu.

"That will take forever!"

"I know, I know," said Amelia Bedelia.

"But we'd better follow Grace's instructions,

or the cookies may not turn out so tasty."

She began to cut each chip in half.

Bits of chocolate flew everywhere.

"This is so silly," said Cousin Alcolu.

"These are not very smart cookies."

"Not smart is right," said Amelia Bedelia.

"These are definitely dumb cookies."

Amelia Bedelia looked at Grace's recipes.

"Gosh," she said. "This is unbelievable.

Grace wants us to bake twelve pound cakes."

"Are you sure?" said Cousin Alcolu.

"Twelve pounds is a mighty heavy cake.

How many twelve-pound cakes

does Grace want us to bake?"

"She didn't say," said Amelia Bedelia.

"Her recipe is for just one pound cake.

One twelve-pound cake should be plenty."

Cousin Alcolu scratched his head.

"Hmmmm," he said.

"If we bake twelve one-pound cakes,

then stack them on top of one another . . . "

"That's it!" said Amelia Bedelia.

"That adds up to a twelve-pound cake.

Cousin Alcolu, you are a genius."

 X 12 =

Amelia Bedelia found twelve pans.

She mixed up a huge bowl of batter.

It was enough for thirteen cakes.

She found another pan and crammed

all thirteen cakes into the oven to bake.

"You know," said Cousin Alcolu,

"a 'baker's dozen' is actually thirteen."

"See there," said Amelia Bedelia.

"You can count better than a baker."

Cousin Alcolu finished cutting

all of the chocolate chips in half.

Then he read the other half of the recipe.

"Please bring me the salt," he said.

"Here you go," said Amelia Bedelia.

She brought him a huge box of salt.

"That is too much," said Cousin Alcolu.

"I just need a pinch."

Amelia Bedelia reached out and . . .

"Ouch!" hollered Cousin Alcolu.

"What did you pinch me for?"

"For the recipe," said Amelia Bedelia.

"I gave you a pinch, like you asked."

Cousin Alcolu rubbed his arm.

"I'm so sorry," said Amelia Bedelia.

"I didn't mean to hurt you.

Now you've got a chip on your shoulder."

"No, I don't," said Cousin Alcolu.

"I'd never hold a grudge against you."

"Hold still," said Amelia Bedelia.

She reached out and plucked

a chocolate chip off his shoulder.

Then she said, "Open wide!"

She tossed the chip into his mouth.

"Yum!" said Cousin Alcolu. "Thanks!"

He finished mixing the dough

and put a batch of cookies

into the second oven to bake.

Amelia Bedelia got three cakes

out of the refrigerator.

"What are those?" asked Cousin Alcolu.

"Grace calls them 'cheesecakes,'"

said Amelia Bedelia.

"We're supposed to put cherries on top."

31

"Cherries with cheese?" said Cousin Alcolu.

"Sounds like a yucky combination to me."

"Me, too," said Amelia Bedelia.

"I bet if these cakes looked cheesier,

they wouldn't need any cherries."

They cut holes

to make a Swiss cheese cake,

drizzled

food coloring

to paint a blue cheese cake,

and planted flags

to create an American cheese cake.

33

Just then, the oven timer went off.

Amelia Bedelia and Cousin Alcolu

took out the pound cakes

and put them on racks to cool.

Then they took the cookies out of the oven

and had a tea break to sample them.

"You know what?" said Amelia Bedelia.

"They taste better with the chips cut in half.

These are smart cookies after all."

"It was worth the work," said Cousin Alcolu.

"Now let's build that twelve-pound cake."

Amelia Bedelia handed him cake after cake.
Cousin Alcolu carefully stacked each one
higher and higher and higher.

"Is it my imagination," said Amelia Bedelia,

"or are the cakes starting to lean?"

"I can't tell," said Cousin Alcolu.

"Hand me that last cake, please."

As soon as he put it on top,

it slid off and crashed onto the table.

"Uh-oh," said Cousin Alcolu.

"This pound cake got pounded."

"No problem," said Amelia Bedelia.

"Our baker's dozen gave us a spare cake.

Bakers must know that accidents happen."

"Lucky for us," said Cousin Alcolu.

Amelia Bedelia checked the recipes.

"Hold on," she said. "This is even luckier.

Grace wants us to make a crumb cake.

Let's just press these crumbs together."

The two of them pushed and prodded

until the crumbs turned into a cake.

"Presto—crumb cake!" said Amelia Bedelia.

"Yessiree," said Cousin Alcolu.

"That is one crummy cake!"

"Uh-oh," said Amelia Bedelia.

"Did we leave something in the oven?"

"That's the phone," said Cousin Alcolu.

"Hello," said Amelia Bedelia.

"This is Grace's Cookie Jar.

May I help you?"

"Hi, it's Grace," said Grace.

"How are things going?"

"Almost done," said Amelia Bedelia.

"We've got one last cake to go,

but I think I'll make it at home."

"Good thinking," said Grace.

"You must be exhausted."

"I am," said Amelia Bedelia.

"I'll bring it in tomorrow."

"I've got an idea," said Grace.

"I'll be at the big Bake-Off.

Just meet me there, okay?"

"Okay," said Amelia Bedelia.

"Thank you! Bye-bye,"

said Grace.

Cousin Alcolu began to clean up.

"I'll handle this mess," he said.

"You go home and bake that cake,

then get some sleep."

"Thank you," said Amelia Bedelia.

"I can barely keep my eyes open."

By the time she got home,
Amelia Bedelia was yawning,
but she had one last cake in her.
It was an old family recipe that
her grandmother had taught her.
There were just nine ingredients.
She mixed them up right in the pan,
then put the pan in the oven.

After the cake had baked and cooled,

she cut two tiny pieces off one end

and set them right on top.

Then she frosted and decorated

her cake from top to bottom.

The next day, Amelia Bedelia overslept.

She was tired from all that baking.

She picked up her cake

and dashed to the Bake-Off.

49

Incredible cakes filled the hall.

Television cameras were everywhere.

Reporters interviewed the bakers.

The excitement was building.

Amelia Bedelia looked around.

She did not see Grace anywhere.

Amelia Bedelia put her cake down on a table

and went to search for her.

At that moment, Chef Du Jour

strolled in Amelia Bedelia's direction.

He looked grumpy, just like on TV.

When he got to Amelia Bedelia's cake,

Chef Du Jour stopped in his tracks.

"What is this?" asked Chef Du Jour.

"Is this someone's idea of a joke?"

"It's my idea,"

said Amelia Bedelia.

"And it is no joke."

"Then what is it?"

demanded the chef.

"It started out as a sheet cake,"

said Amelia Bedelia.

"But I was so tired when I baked it,

I went ahead and made the whole bed."

A smile came over the chef's face.

"It's so easy to make,"

said Amelia Bedelia.

"And it's pretty tasty."

"Really?" said the chef.

"You can actually eat it?"

"Here," said Amelia Bedelia.

"Bite into a pillow."

The chef took a bite.

He closed his eyes and

his smile got even bigger.

"Your cake is simple," he said,

"yet the flavor is complex.

It's funny, but seriously delicious."

"Glad you like it," said Amelia Bedelia.

"Like it?" said Chef Du Jour.

"I love it!

It's fantastic!

Your cake takes the cake,

and first prize!"

There was a huge cheer.

Amelia Bedelia smiled

and waved to everyone at home,

especially the two she knew were watching.

Mr. and Mrs. Rogers were speechless.

Then they jumped for joy.

"See there," said Mrs. Rogers.

"Amelia Bedelia is a smart cookie after all."

"She sure is," said Mr. Rogers.

"And with a thousand dollars,

she's a fortune cookie, too!"

Amelia Bedelia's Sheet Cake

3 cups flour
1 ¾ cups sugar
2 teaspoons baking soda
1 teaspoon salt
⅔ cup cocoa
¾ cup vegetable oil
2 tablespoons vinegar
1 teaspoon vanilla
2 cups water

Step 1
Sift the flour, sugar, baking soda, salt, and cocoa directly into an ungreased 9″ x 13″ pan. Add oil, vinegar, and vanilla. Pour water over all ingredients. Mix with a fork until smooth.

Step 2
Bake at 350 degrees for 25 to 30 minutes.

Step 3
Cool the cake and ice it in the pan with your favorite frosting.